Written by: Junior and Reba McLaughlin

Illustrations by: Blueberry Illustrations

Creativity Director: Bob Ennis

Assistant Creativity Director: Nancy Ennis

Content Editor: Amy Betz

Buster would like to personally thank
his excellent team of test marketers:
Cady, Gabe, Wesley, Oliver, Alice, Henry, Joy, Camy,
Olivia, Cannon, Caris, Addie Kate, Mikiyas, and Eliana

Farmer Bob could always find a use for things that other people had thrown away. His mailbox was made from an old milk can and the weathervane on top of his barn was made from a broom.

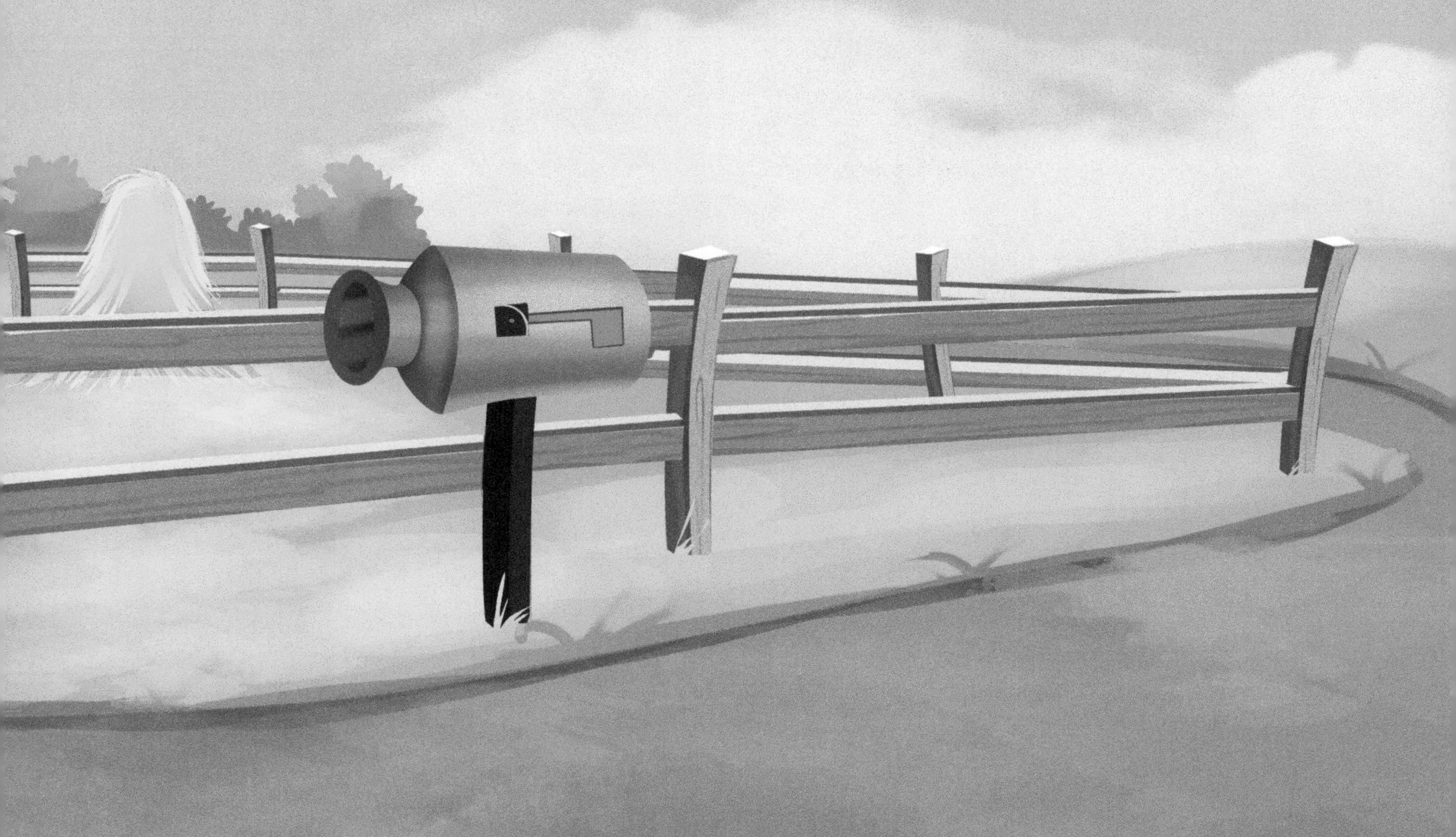

Farmer Bob's chickens, Clara and Beatrice, didn't even have a normal chicken coop! Instead, they laid their eggs in an old clothes dryer with a slanted roof.

Buster was a friendly brown horse who lived on Farmer Bob's farm. He ate his hay from an old laundry basket.

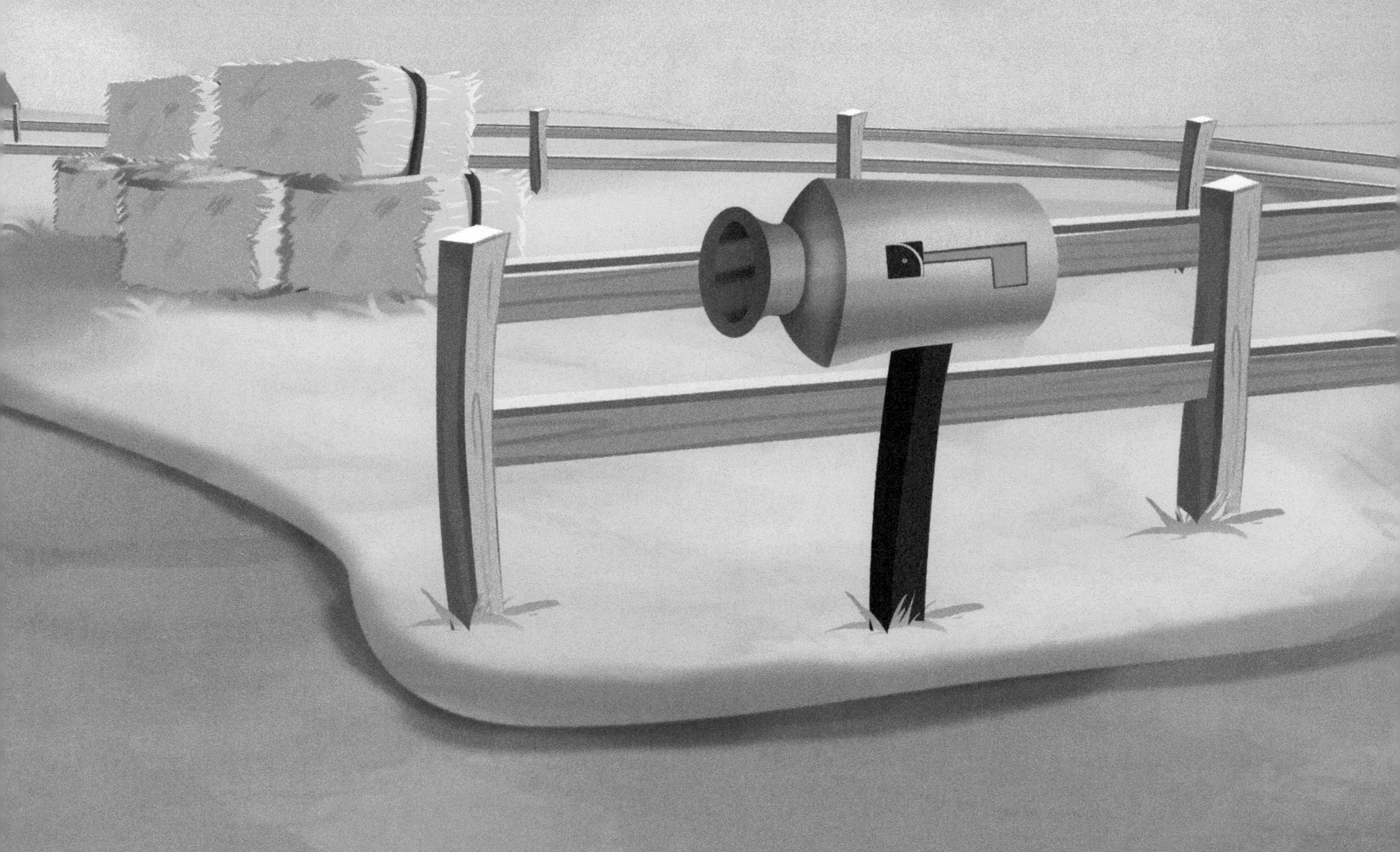

Buster's best friend was Annabelle, Farmer Bob's daughter.
Annabelle visited Buster every day after school.
They loved to chase the chickens, and
they waved at anyone who passed by.

Every afternoon, kids rode
their bikes past the farm.
They shouted, "Hi, Buster! Hi,
Annabelle!" as they whizzed by.

HAPPY BIRTHDAY

One afternoon, Buster was the guest of honor at Annabelle's seventh birthday party. He even helped her blow out the candles on her birthday cake.

Annabelle got exactly what
she wanted for her birthday:
a brand-new pink bike with
a basket and a bell.

The next day, Annabelle was late for her usual visit with Buster. He was worried. He felt lonely when the kids rode their bikes by his pasture.

"Hi, Buster!"
the kids said as
they rode past.

Buster couldn't believe it
when he saw the last kid go by.

It was Annabelle riding her new pink bike.

"Hi, Buster!" she said as she rode off with the other kids.

Buster was sad. He missed his best friend.

Then he had an idea.

"I'm going to learn how to ride a bike too," Buster thought. "I just have to find one. Maybe Farmer Bob has one in his workshop."

The next morning, Buster went into Farmer Bob's workshop. Sure enough, there was an old bike propped up against the wall.

Every morning,
Buster went into the
big red barn and tried
to learn how to ride
that old bike.

Buster tried and tried but he could not learn how to ride the bike.

“This bike has two pedals and I’ve got four legs,” Buster thought. “I need to figure out a way to make this work.”

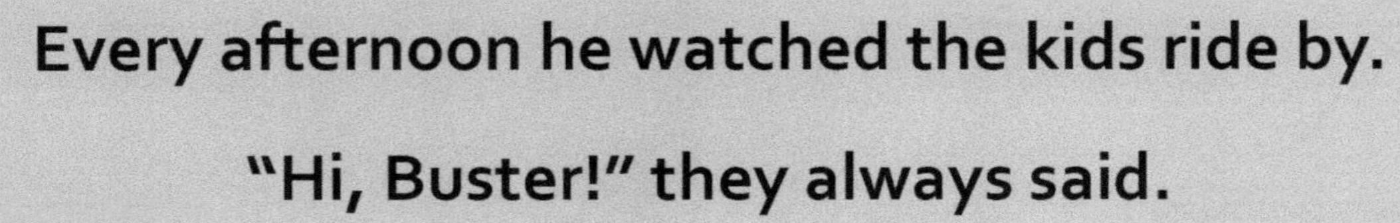

Every afternoon he watched the kids ride by.

"Hi, Buster!" they always said.

One day, Annabelle noticed that Buster looked unhappy. She was also very sad and missed spending time with her best friend.

That evening
Annabelle asked
Farmer Bob if he
thought Buster was
OK. "He looked sad
when I rode by today,"
she told him.

Annabelle's dad was a wise man. He had spotted Buster in the big red barn trying to ride the old bike.

"I've got an idea," he told Annabelle. "Tomorrow is Saturday, so you don't have school. Meet me in my workshop when you finish your chores. Maybe we can make a bike for Buster."

Annabelle woke up extra early the next morning to get all her chores done. She fed the chickens and pigs, and then she ran to the workshop where she found her dad hard at work building a very unusual bike.

This bike had parts of an old barrel at the front, and the front tire was an old wagon wheel. Instead of two pedals like a normal bike, this bike had four!

"You're building
Buster a double bike!"
Annabelle exclaimed.

Annabelle and her father
worked all morning on
Buster's special bike.

HAPPY BIRTHDAY
HAPPY BIRTHDAY

A few days later, it was Buster's birthday.

Annabelle invited all her friends. She was so excited to give Buster the present she had made with her father.

She drew Buster a birthday card. Inside she wrote, "To my best friend, Buster. Now we can ride bikes together."

Happy Birthday
Buster
To my best
friend,
Buster!

Buster was so happy when he saw the double bike. He couldn't wait to ride it.

At first, he wobbled, but before long he was proudly riding around his pasture.

"I knew I would ride a bike someday," Buster thought to himself.

HappyBirthda
Buster

The kids at the party
were all amazed that
Buster had learned
to ride a double bike.

"Wow, Buster! Now you can ride bikes with us," the kids all said. "We are going to have so many fun adventures. Let's go!"

Annabelle was so happy to be able to
spend time with her best friend again.

ISBN: 978-0-578-88746-3